# Branta and the Golden Stone

# Branta and the Golden Stone

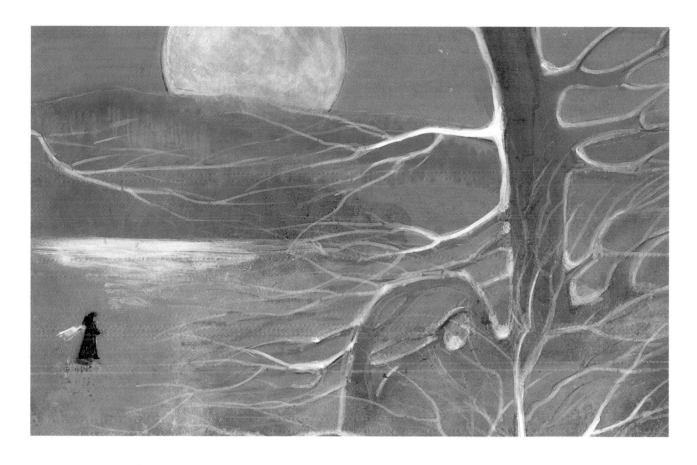

By Walter Wangerin, Jr.
Illustrated by Deborah Healy

SIMON & SCHUSTER BOOKS FOR YOUNG READERS
Published by Simon & Schuster
New York    London    Toronto    Sydney    Tokyo    Singapore

SIMON & SCHUSTER BOOKS FOR YOUNG READERS
Simon & Schuster Building, Rockefeller Center, 1230 Avenue of the Americas, New York, New York 10020
Text copyright © 1993 by Walter M. Wangerin, Jr. Illustrations copyright © 1993 by Deborah Healy
All rights reserved including the right of reproduction in whole or in part in any form.
SIMON & SCHUSTER BOOKS FOR YOUNG READERS is a trademark of Simon & Schuster.
Designed by Vicki Kalajian. The text of this book is set in 14 point ITC Garamond Light.
The illustrations were done as oil paintings. Manufactured in the United States of America

10    9    8    7    6    5    4    3    2    1

*Library of Congress Cataloging-in-Publication Data*
Wangerin, Walter. Branta and the golden stone / by Walter Wangerin ;
illustrated by Deborah Healy.    Summary: Alone on an island at the top of the world,
Branta uses a magic golden stone to save a family of geese from freezing to death.  [1. Magic—Fiction.
2. Geese—Fiction.]   I. Healy, Deborah, ill.   II. Title.  PZ7.W1814Br  1993  [Fic]—dc20  92-34891  CIP
ISBN: 0-671-79693-3

*To my mother
the poet
Virginia*

WW

*For my mother Ruth, and my family
Edward, Jane and John.
Also for my generous friend Edna Doll,
and my Moore students for their good comments.*

DH

Once there was a girl who lived alone on the northernmost island in all the world.

She lived in a cottage by a lake. The lake was ice for most of the year, banked with snow. Her father had built the cottage long ago. It had two rooms and a fireplace, a table, a chair, a little window that faced the lake, and in each room a little bed.

The girl had flashing black eyes and midnight hair tied back from her brow. Her neck was noble, her skin so dark it gleamed in the moonlight—and always she wore a snow-white scarf buttoned above her ears.

If she walked abroad in the snow, you could see her because of her dark skin.

If she walked abroad at night, you could see her because of her scarf.

Her name was Branta.

And often that winter she walked abroad. She left the cottage and wandered across the frozen lake exactly as the moon goes wandering across the sky. Branta was lonely.

Her father had died a year ago.

He had been a big man once, with a wild white beard and tremendous arms for carrying firewood. Branta's father had always kept a fire in the fireplace. No matter how cold the winter grew, their cottage was warm and bright and lovely.

But then one morning the man didn't get out of bed.

Branta had knocked on his door. "Papa?" she whispered. "Papa?" But all she heard was a moaning like wind in the trees. She opened the door and saw by his eyes that her father was very sick.

All day long she bathed his face. He seemed to be sleeping. He seemed to be fighting inside his dreams. For her father's sake, Branta kept the fire bright and warm in the fireplace.

Then in the evening he called to her. "Branta."

"What, Papa?"

"Sit beside me," he whispered. "I have something to tell you."

She sat and bent her noble neck toward him. He closed his eyes and spoke.

"You've never asked why we live so far north," he said.

"I never minded," said Branta.

"Once," said the man with the wild white beard, "when your mother and I were young and happy, I was a *magus*—a wise man—Branta. I could read the stars in heaven as if they were words on a page. But then," he whispered very softly, "I stole the Golden Stone, and it made me famous. It made me more than a *magus*. It made me a magician."

"Papa?" said Branta. "Why didn't you tell me these things before?"

He opened his eyes and looked at his daughter. "Because I am ashamed of them," he said. "They made your mother sad."

"But then why are you telling me now?"

"Because I must give you something before I die," he said, "and you must understand it."

"Die?" said Branta. "Oh, Papa, let's talk of other things. Here, let me go build the fire for you—"

"No, let the fire grow cold!" her father commanded. "Stay with me and listen!"

Far, far into the night then, while the fire dwindled to ash and the gray ash cooled, Branta's father told her his story.

"The most important message I ever read in the stars," he said, "was that a Baby King was to be born in a distant kingdom. When I told it to your mother, she said, 'Go. Who else can read the stars as you do? Who else knows that the Baby King is coming? Yet someone must welcome him. Go.'

"So my brothers took spices from orient trees as gifts, and I took a stone of gold for the Baby King. We traveled the deserts westward. Finally, we found the tiny child, and I knew at once he was more than a baby and more than a king.

"He gazed at us from his mother's arms. He raised his hands and blessed us. My brothers put their spices on the ground before him, but I lifted my gift to the child himself. He reached and touched it. Branta, listen: Where his finger touched the gold it made a deep print; and the whole stone glowed hot in my hand, and I felt power go into it!

"Branta, Branta, I never let go of that stone. And when no one was looking, I slipped it into my pouch. My brothers brought frankincense and myrrh and left them there. I brought gold and took it back again. I stole the Golden Stone and the print of the Baby King's finger."

Tears flowed from the old man's eyes now, but he kept on talking.

"Your mother was frightened when she saw what I had done. 'Take it back,' she said. 'It belongs to the Baby King!'

"I said, 'But if the Good King touched it, it will do good for many people.'

"She said, 'Please, please, take it back.'

"But I didn't. I used it. And, indeed, I did much good with it. For this was the power of the Golden Stone, that it changed people. It made them whatever they wanted to be. It made sick people healthy, it gave sight to the blind, it caused the crippled to walk. And often I said to your mother, 'Do you see all the good I'm doing?'

"But she said, 'No, husband. I see instead that the Golden Stone has changed you, too. Now you are what you always wanted to be, a magician proud and famous. And that is not good.'

"Your mother's words made me angry. So I said, 'Woman, be still!'

"She looked at me and said, 'Do you mean that?'

"'Shut up! Shut up!' I shouted. 'Woman, don't talk to me!'

"Well, then your mother went to the place where I kept the Golden Stone. She put her finger on the Baby King's print, and she whispered, 'You have your wish. It is my wish, too. I will never speak again.'

"In the days that followed, your mother did not speak, and I continued my work with the Golden Stone. People came and were changed.

"Did an angry man want to be fire to burn his enemy's house? When he left he was a pure white flame, and his enemy's house burned down, indeed—but the man himself was never seen again.

"Did a greedy man wish to be rain to get himself rich crops? Well, he became a wonderful rainstorm, and his fields brought forth abundantly—but someone else harvested them, because this man had run in streams to the sea.

"Do you hear the danger of the Golden Stone, Branta?" the old man asked. "No, no, it wasn't all goodness. Whatever the people became, they had to stay that way forever. If someone wished silence for a little while—well, the silence lasted forever. Is the fire out yet," he whispered. "Is the grating cold yet?"

Quietly, Branta rose and went to the fireplace. "Yes," she said. "It is out."

"Your mother died in silence," the man said. Branta could not see him in the darkness. It sounded as if he were speaking from far away. "She was going to have a baby. She lay down in silence. In silence she bore a baby girl. And in silence she died. Branta, you were that baby girl.

"Branta?" the old man called. "Branta, can you hear me?"

But she could not speak now, because of her sadness. She could only nod.

Her father said, "Reach into the ashes. Do you feel something hard and smooth?"

Yes, she felt a stone the size of a sparrow's egg.

"Please bring it here," he said, and Branta did. She carried to her father a stone of gold so pure it glowed upon their faces. In its center was a baby's fingerprint.

"When your mother died, I tried to find the King to return his stone," the old man whispered. "But that was years later, and no one knew of such a king. So I went away. I brought us to the northernmost island in the world, and I built a little cottage, and I built a big fire to keep you warm, and I loved you, child, and I tried…" The old man closed his eyes.

Branta waited for him to draw his next breath, but he never did. Her father's beard was like the night cloud round his face. He was peaceful now, and he was dead.

So that's why Branta lived alone by the lake. And that's why she walked abroad all winter long in loneliness. She was thinking about her father.

When the nights were still, she would button the white scarf above her ears and go forth like the moon. When blizzards struck her island, blowing and shrieking and piling snow against the cottage, she stayed inside, building fires bright and warm.

But every night, whether windy or still, she would touch the Golden Stone, which now she kept in the center of her father's pillow as a memorial to him.

*T*he northernmost island in all the world is winter for most of the year. But finally there comes a brief spring when the ice breaks and the water gurgles down to the lake and the flowers sprout and grow.

And so it was that the winter of Branta's sadness suddenly came to an end when company came to her island awhile.

One morning, while the water still dripped from the eaves of her cottage, Branta stepped outside and looked around. She thought she'd heard somebody laughing.

The lake was glittering, the hills were green, the sky was bright and perfectly blue; but there was nobody anywhere, nobody laughing—

All at once she heard it again. Straight up in the sky so high they were invisible, *two* somebodies were chatting and laughing and telling jokes in nasal voices: *"Gaba-gaba-gaba!"* they said.

"Who are you?" Branta cried.

And then, exactly as if in answer to her question, she saw in the distance two dark bodies with points in front and streaks at their sides, which Branta took to be wings.

"Birds," she whispered.

They began to spiral down toward her island, great birds with black faces and long necks, pure white markings at their throats, gray bodies, and wings of a powerful stroke.

"Why, you are geese!" cried Branta, and she raised her hands for gladness. "Geese! Geese, I hope you will land on my lake!"

And they did!

Down they sailed on outstretched wings—splendid, regal creatures. They made a circle over the water, then pulled up on the flap of a wing, bent their necks, put out their feet, skated the surface, and sank and sat and twitched their tails, curving their noble necks. A long journey was done.

"Geese!" cried Branta. "Geese, tell me a joke and I will laugh with you!"

But the goose and her gander only glanced once at the girl on the shore; then they paddled to the other side of the lake, where they chatted and groomed their feathers.

"*Gaba-gaba-gaba,*" they said—no language Branta could understand, no joke that she could laugh at. For geese are geese and people are people. They can be neighbors sharing a lake, but they cannot talk or hug as fathers and daughters do.

"But you don't mind if I watch you, do you?" Branta murmured.

*Gaba-gaba-gaba.* From their distance, the geese didn't seem to mind at all.

Branta took comfort in that. Life had returned to her island. And so the summer was good to her, and she was glad.

Flowers burst in red and blue. The grass grew long all around the lake. The female goose made a nest in the tall green shade, and in her nest she laid six eggs; and the gander and she made comfortable cluckings both day and night, and Branta was filled with excitement. In all her life she had never seen babies before.

So then the eggs hatched. And here came six brave goslings, each a puffball the size of Branta's fist, all following their mother, peeping, charging the waves of the lake, and rowing out like tiny boats.

Branta laughed aloud on the shore, and sometimes the baby geese glanced in her direction, and then she laughed harder than ever—as if she had the right to feel proud of such handsome babies.

But swiftly do babies grow up. Soon the goslings were gone and six true geese had taken their places, six faces black-and-white, six necks as noble as their parents' necks, six pairs of wings now strong for flight, and six new voices calling "*Gaba-gaba-gaba*" in laughter Branta could not join, in language she couldn't understand.

The summer was over. Eight grown geese would soon depart. Branta began to prepare for winter, carrying firewood into the cottage as her father had done before her and stiffening her heart for the loneliness soon to come again.

$\mathcal{B}$ut this was the northernmost island in all the world. Winter can come here so suddenly that even geese might be caught by surprise.

In the year after Branta's father died, that is exactly what happened. One night summer died. A storm tore down from the northern seas and beat against her cottage all night long.

When she crept to her window in the morning, Branta saw that the grass was broken and frozen in ice, the sky was low and blowing, and the lake had been lashed to a foaming black fury. The north wind blew and blew—and there, huddled behind a boulder bigger than they, were the geese!

"Oh, no!" cried Branta. "I thought you were gone! Dear geese, you can hardly walk in this weather—however will you fly?"

All day Branta watched the family from her window, but the wind didn't break and the geese didn't move. And then the night arrived in perfect darkness, and the wind blew so fiercely that the fire in her fireplace cowered and guttered out.

On the second day of the storm it snowed. The lake stayed black; but the ground grew thick with drifts, and the geese were swallowed altogether.

"Where are you?" Branta called. She buttoned the white scarf above her ears and ran out into the blizzard. "Are you dead?" She stumbled toward the boulder, which was now sunken in snow. "Please, please," she cried, "don't die!"

Branta reached into the snowdrift and touched warm feathers. Immediately, eight geese burst up in a shower of snow and began to race away from her. Branta chased them.

"Wait," she called. "I want to help you!"

But they were afraid of her! They were as scared of Branta as they were of the storm. When she ran at the gander, he opened his wings to fly from her; but the wind slapped him backward, and he rolled like a snowball along the ground. She tried to grab him. "Come with me," she begged. "You'll die out here."

But it was no good. The gander stuck his face in the wind and with a desperate beating of his wings moved farther and farther away. So did they all. Branta had visions of eight geese frozen in the cold, their black eyes closed or clouded. Yet whenever she drew near to them, they ran faster and farther away.

*So then,* thought Branta, *maybe I could scare them into the cottage!* She began to wave her arms and to scream louder than the wind. "Go! Go! Go!" she screamed—and for a little while the plan worked. The geese ran in front of her. She aimed them toward the door of her cottage, the warmth of the fire—

But at the last instant they split and raced around the cottage, farther and farther away.

"Oh, you stupid geese!" Branta wept. She stopped and leaned against the cottage wall. "You have to come inside. The cold is going to kill you, don't you know?" What could she possibly do to save them?

"*Gaba-gaba-gaba!*" said the gander. And then, no matter how tired his family was, no matter how windy the world or how cold, they gathered all around him. "*Gaba-gaba-gaba,*" he said—and suddenly Branta knew exactly what she would do.

She walked into the cottage. She knelt before the fire to be sure there was plenty of wood to last a long, long time. Then she rose and went into her father's room.

At his bedside she reached for the Golden Stone still on his pillow, and she held it in the palm of her hand awhile, gazing at the tiny fingerprint.

"Baby King," she said, "I want to be a goose."

Branta placed the Golden Stone on her tongue. It was small. It tasted like spices, bitter and sweet and powerful.

Then she swallowed it.

For a moment she kept her head bowed in silence. Then a fire rose in her heart, which became a blazing brand. It coursed through her veins to the surface of her flesh, and she bent down, she bent her long neck down—and when she raised it up again, Branta was a goose, a bright and glowing goose, for the heat went out from her body into the air.

Now she went back the way that she had come. She took short steps, silly, waddling steps, out into the storm—but the cold did not sting her anymore. She walked through drifts to the back of the cottage, calling *"Gaba-gaba-gaba!"* Here and there various geese poked their heads up through the snow, looking for the source of the cry.

*"Gather-gather-gather,"* called Branta the goose, nipping the younger geese on the backs of their necks. Some of them had already tucked their heads beneath their wings, preparing to sleep and to die. Branta would not allow it. *"Gaba-gaba-get up!"* she scolded them.

The mother of the children was staring into the darkness, nearly dead with cold. But when she saw Branta—somebody exactly her size and shape, with the same white markings under her throat and the same black beak—well, she stood up and followed. Of course! Why wouldn't one goose trust and follow another goose who spoke the exact same language, after all?

And the gander said, *"Gaba-gaba-Branta!"* He called her by name. *"Good-for-you-ba-Branta,"* he said, and then he was the last of the family of geese to follow her into the cottage; and there they all spent the third night of the storm, close to a fire both warm and bright. And so it was that they survived.

*W*hen finally the storm abated that year and the sun returned to warm the earth awhile, a flock of geese flew up from the northernmost island in all the world. They formed a perfect *V* and turned toward the south. It was late in the season to be leaving, but these geese were no less healthy nor strong for that.

Soon they were gossiping and telling jokes. Soon they were laughing, as do all geese when they travel.

*"Gaba-gaba-gaba!"* they said.

There were nine in the flock: six children flying their first flight south, a mother goose and a gander, too—and one that had once been a girl, Branta, laughing as freely as any goose.

For this was the truth of the Golden Stone, the length of love and the fullness of sacrifice: that whatever a person chose to become, she would stay that way forever.